DC SUPER
FRIENDS
™

GOING
BANANAS

D0302296
3 0116 01873496 0

GOING BANANAS
A BANTAM BOOK 978 0 857 51186 7

Published in Great Britain by Bantam, an imprint of Random House Children's Publishers UK
A Random House Group Company

This edition published 2013

1 3 5 7 9 10 8 6 4 2

RHUK 28472

Bantam Books are published by Random House Children's Publishers UK,
61–63 Uxbridge Road, London W5 5SA

www.**randomhousechildrens**.co.uk

Addresses for companies within The Random House Group Limited can be found at:
www.randomhouse.co.uk/offices.htm

THE RANDOM HOUSE GROUP Limited Reg. No. 954009

A CIP catalogue record for this book is available from the British Library

Printed in China

The Random House Group Limited supports The Forest Stewardship Council® (FSC®), the leading international forest certification organization. Our books carrying the FSC label are printed on FSC®-certified paper. FSC is the only forest certification scheme endorsed by the leading environmental organizations, including Greenpeace. Our paper procurement policy can be found at www.randomhouse.co.uk/environment

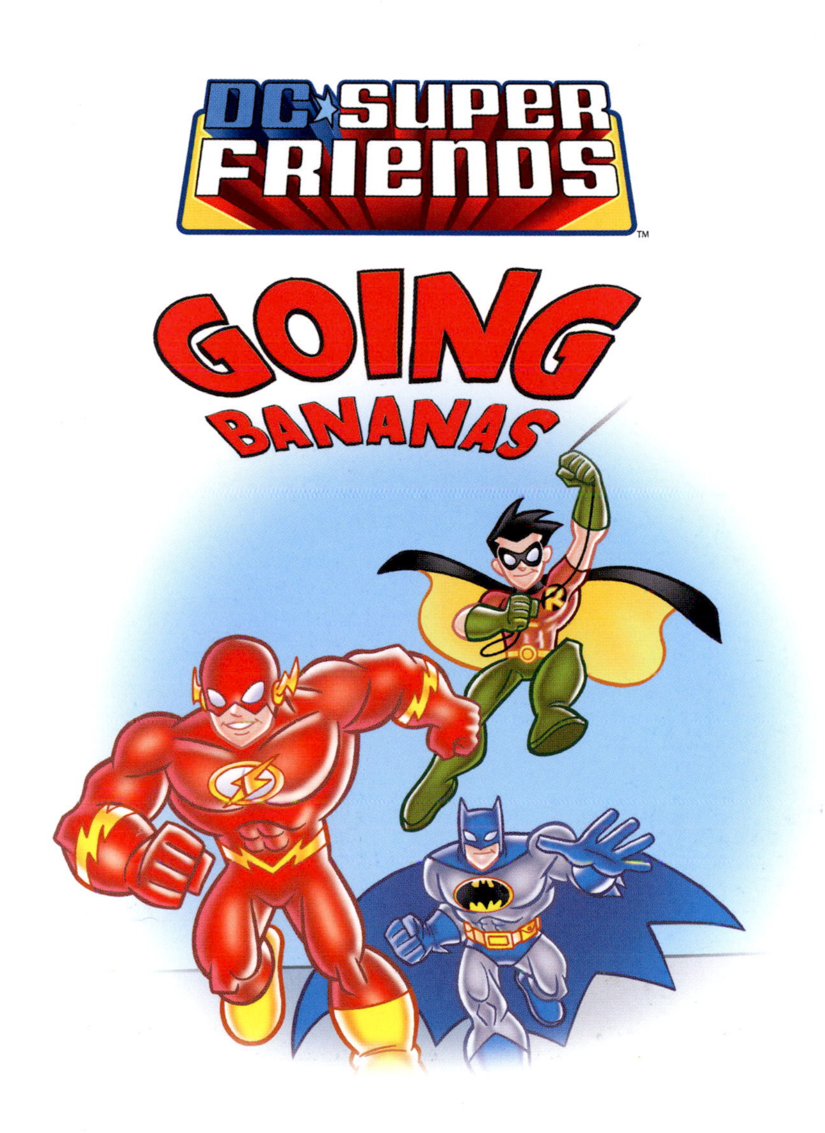

By Benjamin Harper
Illustrated by Erik Doescher,
Mike DeCarlo and David Tanguay

BANTAM BOOKS

Metropolis is having
a precious gems show.

Everyone wants to see the big yellow diamond!

The diamond is gone!
Without it, the show
cannot open.

The Super Friends
will help!
They will find
the diamond.

Superman uses
his X-ray vision.
He finds a clue!

Green Lantern
finds another clue!
He spots some
strange fingerprints.

Across town,
there is trouble
at the docks.

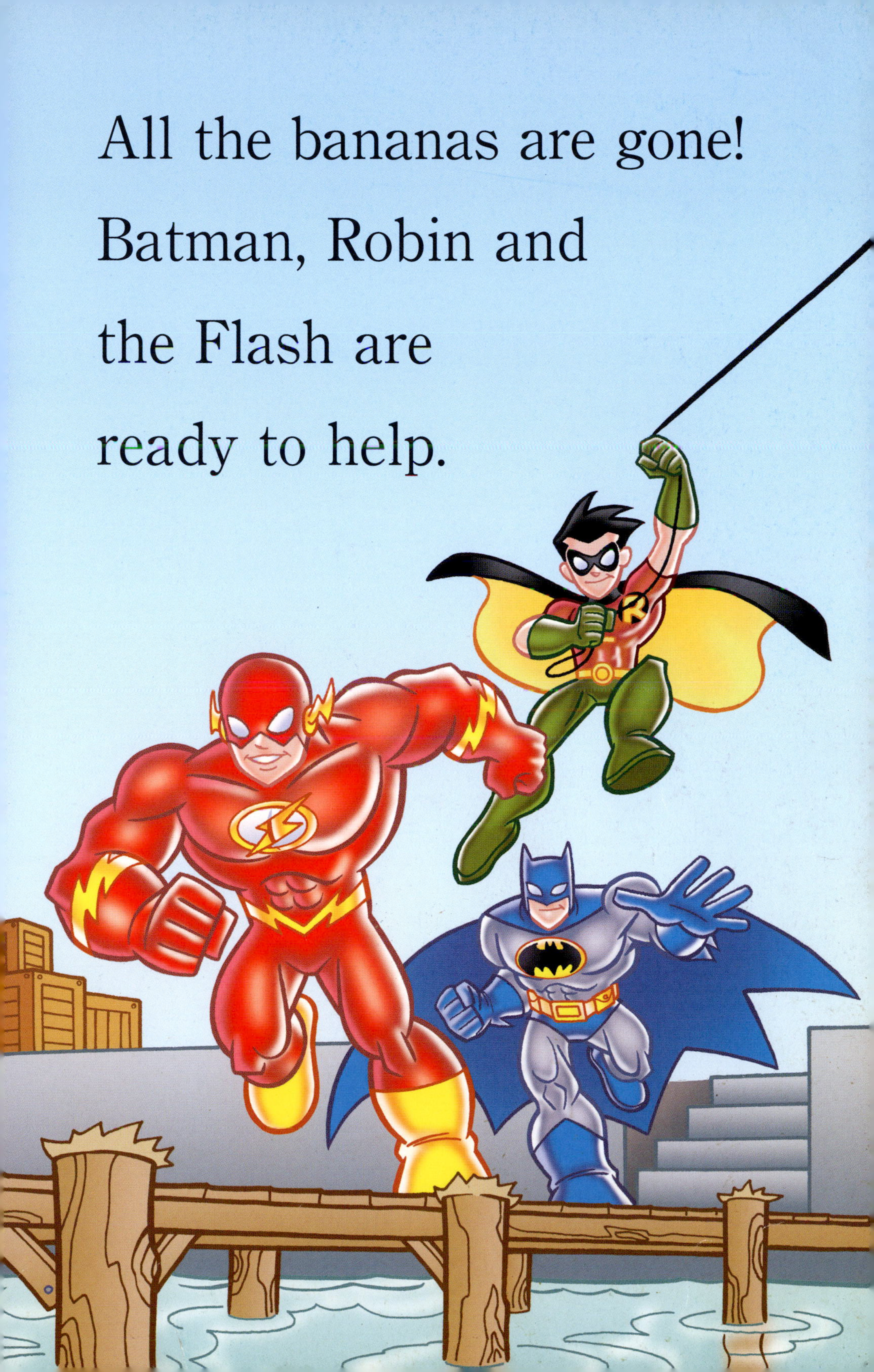

All the bananas are gone!
Batman, Robin and
the Flash are
ready to help.

Batman spots
more strange
fingerprints!

Superman sees even

more trouble.

A truck full of bananas

has been stolen!

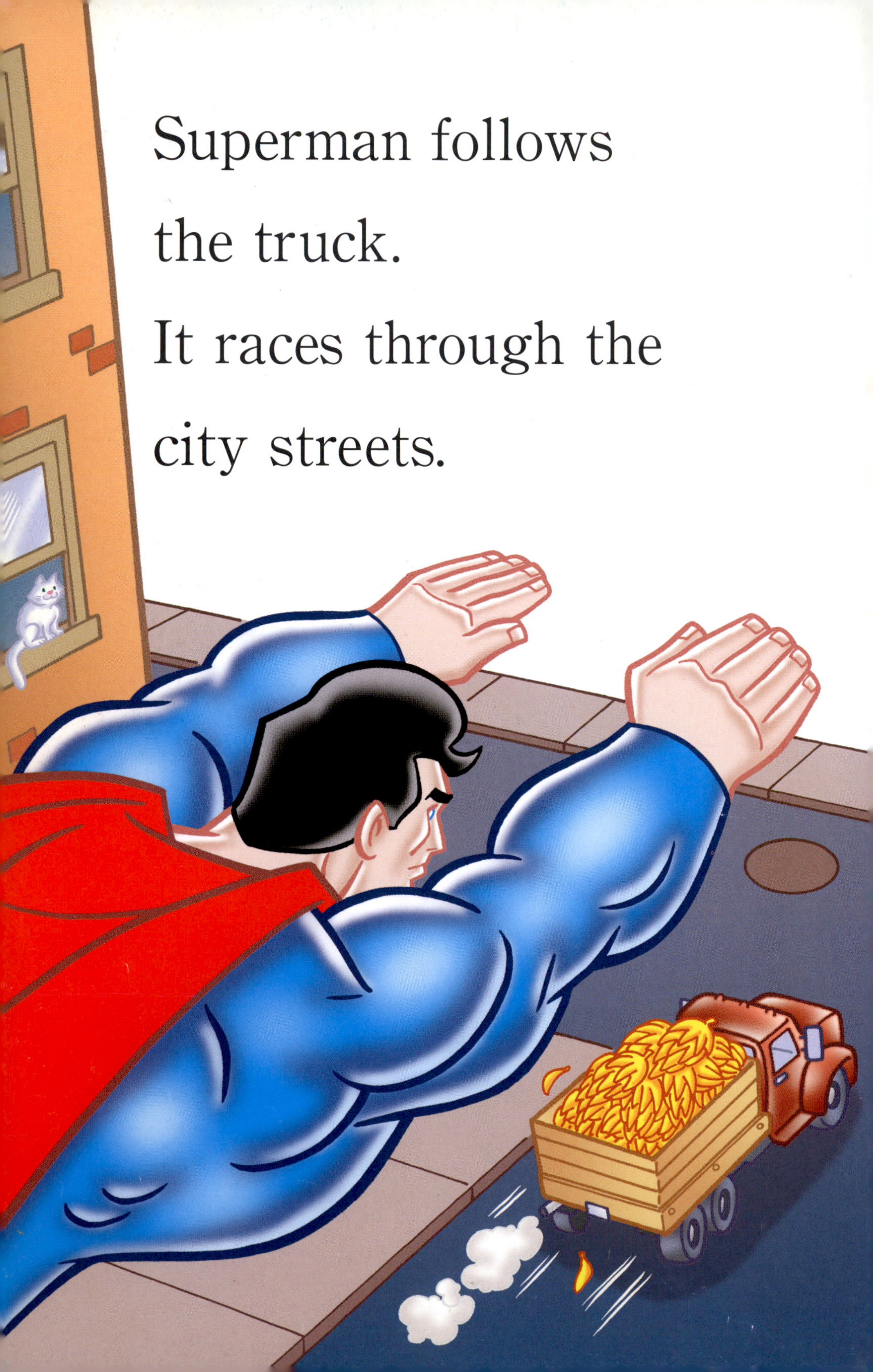

Superman follows
the truck.
It races through the
city streets.

The truck stops.
A gorilla gets out!
Superman takes
a closer look.

It is Gorilla Grodd!
He's using a magic box,
the diamond and
some bananas.

He is making
a magical
gorilla army.

"You are too late!"
Grodd says.

“My gorillas will
take over the city.
And then we will
take over the world!”

Gorillas go everywhere!
They run in the park.
They jump into the pond.

The Flash ties up
a gorilla with
some rope!
Cyborg helps him.

Gorillas run wild!

They make a mess.

Robin and Green Lantern
trap the gorillas.
They cannot go
anywhere!

Superman works fast.

The gorillas turn back

into bananas!

Batman captures Grodd.

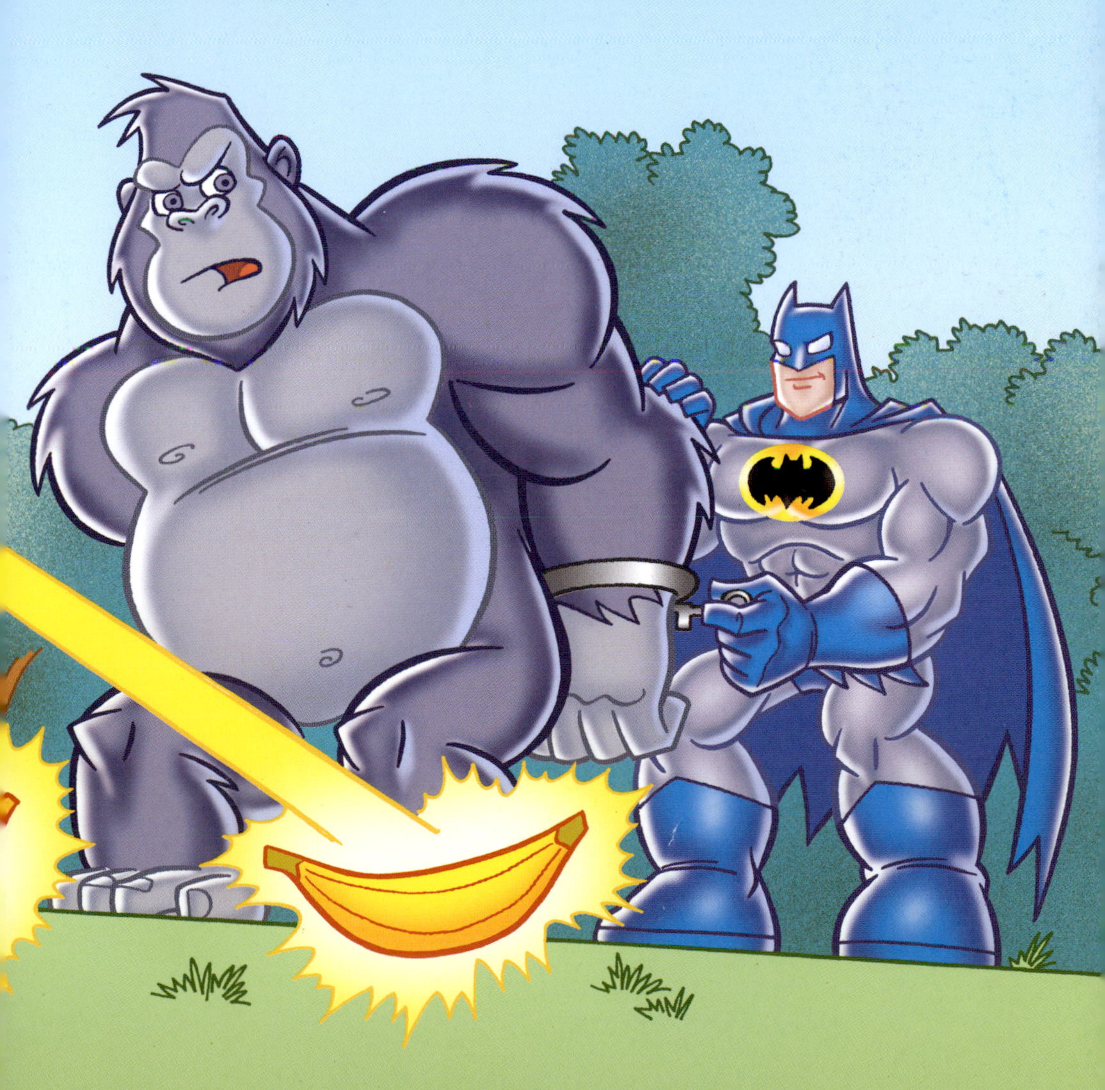

Roar!

Grodd breaks free.

He grabs the diamond.

He escapes!

Superman chases Grodd.

He must not get away!

Gorilla Grodd hides at the zoo.

Which gorilla has the diamond?

Superman knows!

Growl!

Gorilla Grodd cannot

hide any more.

He is taken away.

The Super Friends
return the diamond
just in time.
The show can go on!

The precious gems show is a hit – thanks to the Super Friends!

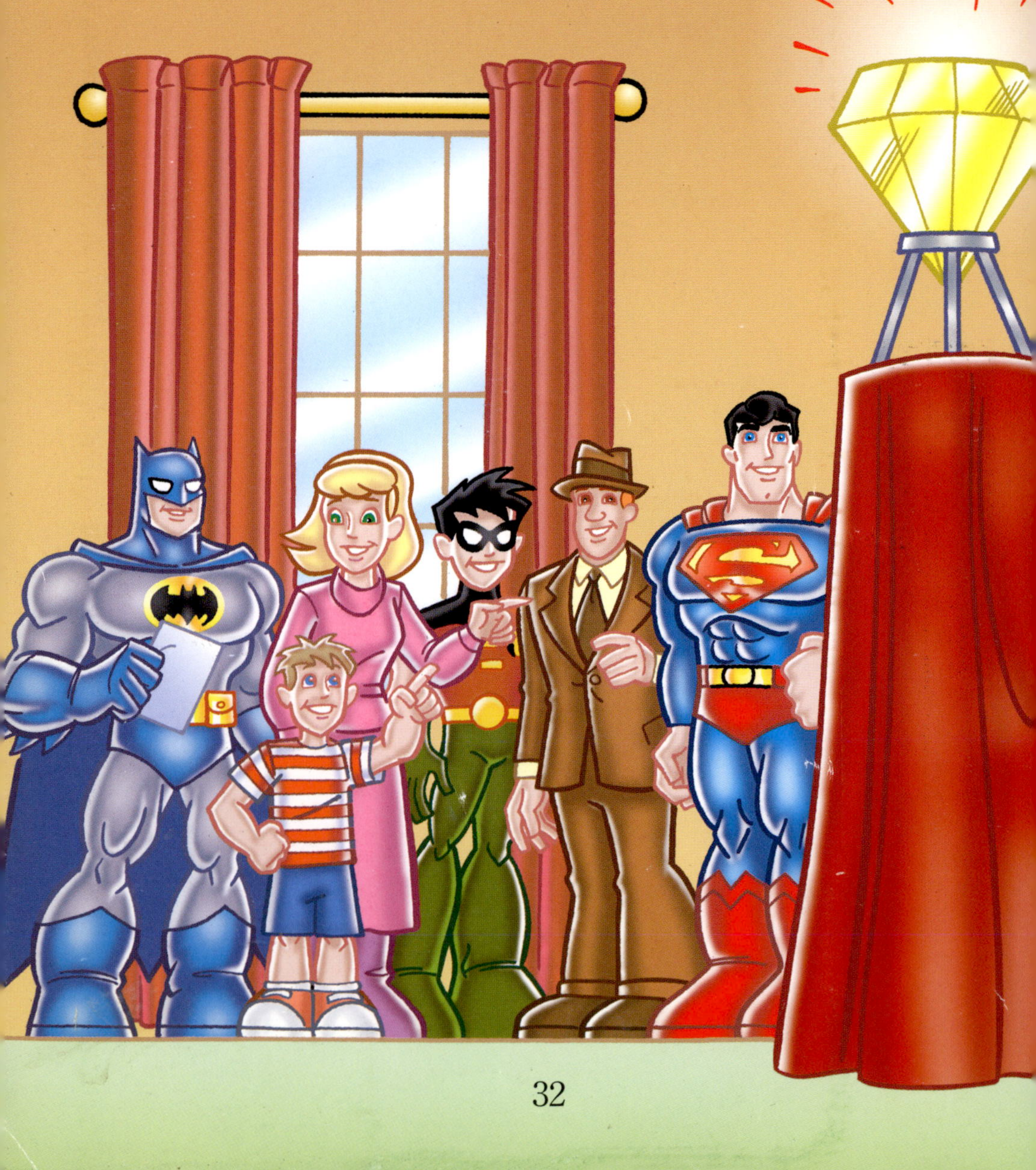